The Little Country Town

N SOUTHWELL

The Little Country Town

illustrated by

KAY CHORAO

Henry Holt and Company ❧ New York

Henry Holt and Company, LLC
Publishers since 1866
115 West 18th Street
New York, New York 10011

Henry Holt is a registered trademark of Henry Holt and Company, LLC

Published in Canada by Fitzhenry & Whiteside Ltd., 195 Allstate Parkway,
Markham, Ontario L3R 4T8.

Library of Congress Cataloging-in-Publication Data
Southwell, Jandelyn
The little country town / by Jandelyn Southwell; illustrated by Kay Chorao.
Summary: When the sun sets on a quiet country town, the nighttime sounds and scents begin.
[1. Night–Fiction. 2. Country life–Fiction. 3. Stories in rhyme.]
I. Chorao, Kay, ill. II. Title.
PZ8.3.S72 Li 2000   [E]–dc21   99-53628

ISBN 0-8050-5711-0 / First Edition–2000
The artist used gouache on watercolor paper to create the illustrations for this book.
Designed by Martha Rago
Printed in the United States of America on acid-free paper. ∞
1 3 5 7 9 10 8 6 4 2

To Justin, Alexander, and Drake
for being the inspiration in all I do
–J. S.

To the North Fork,
and especially Jamesport, Long Island
–K. C.

In a quiet country town,

by a dusty little road,

there's a great green field

where the wildflowers grow.

And each and every night,
when the sun goes down,

you can smell their sweet scent
in the little country town.

On the dusty little road,
there's a crooked covered bridge,

and a stream of crystal water,

where the little froggies live.

And each and every night,
when the sun goes down,

you can hear the froggies croaking
in the little country town.

In the great grassy field

grows a big and mighty tree,

with strong and sturdy branches

and lush green leaves.

And each and every night,
when the sun goes down,

you can hear the leaves rustling
in the little country town.

On a long lean branch
lies a nest of speckled birds,

who sing the sweetest songs
that the town has ever heard.

And each and every night,
as the sun goes down,

you can hear the birds cheeping
in the little country town.

As the day comes to an end
and fireflies appear,

crickets start to chirp
and the night draws near.

And each and every night,
when the sun goes down,

the stars shine brightly
on the little country town.

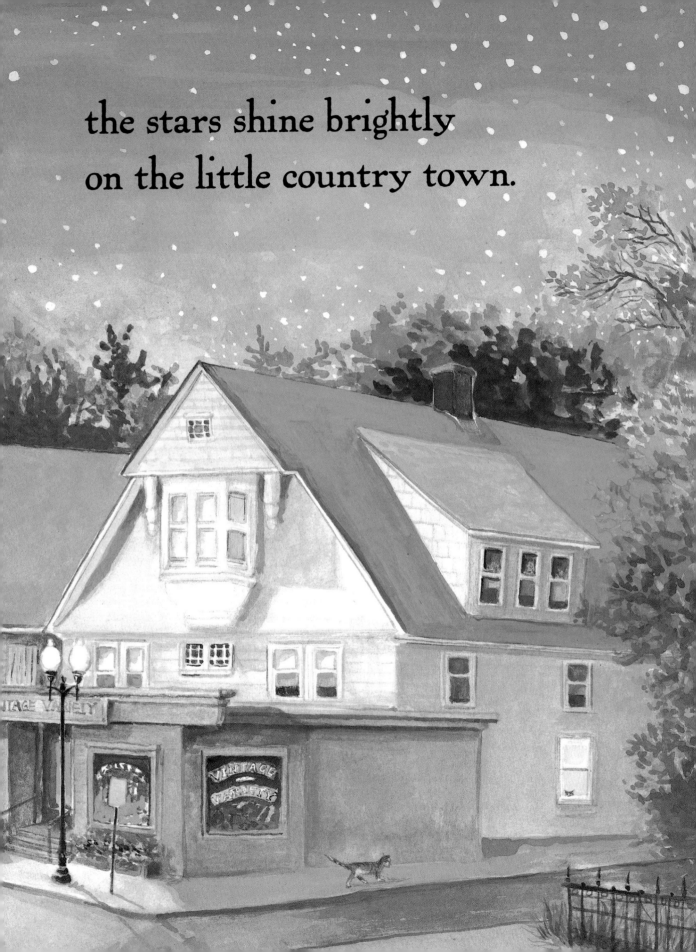